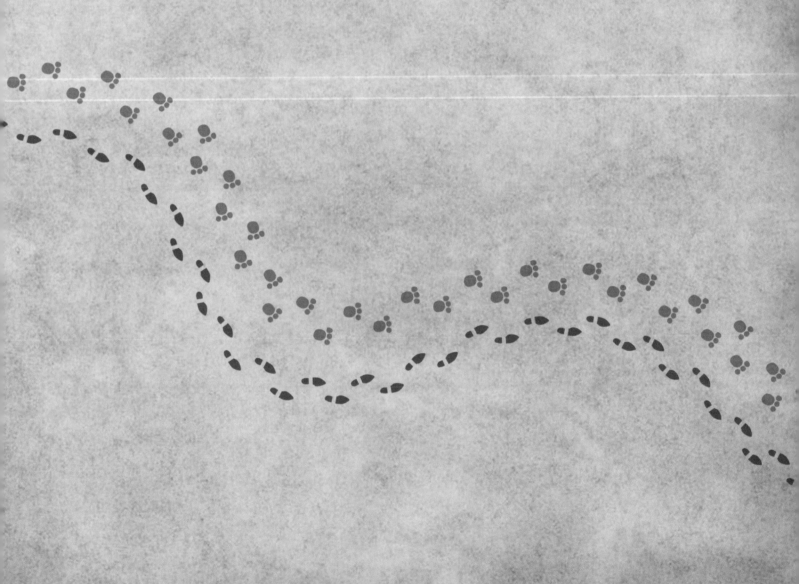

A VERY IMPORTANT POWER

By Wild West Wendy Jo

VIPPI TREASURE QUESTS™

Illustrated by
Tobias White & Wendy Jo Bradshaw

A
REALLY
REALLY
IMPORTANT POWER!

For everyone who has ever felt like
they didn't matter or belong.

CONTENTS

1 — THE BEGINNING

As the western sun was setting on their *Vippi Treasure Quest Show* stage, the quirky TV show duo of *Wild West Wendy Jo* and *Vippi Mouse,* were about to *decide* which *treasure* hunting destination they would guide kids to next.

Wild West Wendy Jo, also known as The Singing Cowgirl, picked the *map* up, and had an idea. She said, "What better adventure than to show kids where it all began?" The feisty, redhead, grinned at her old *friend* and asked, "Do you remember back when I was a child and we first met?"

"Of course, Wendy Jo, how could I forget?" the fun-loving, TV host mouse exclaimed. Vippi turned to the TV audience, "Hey kids! Let's take a walk down memory lane." Heads together, they leaned forward, peered into Vippi's *magic* magnifying glass and looked back in *time*.

Wyoming 1968

Wendy Jo was in her childhood farmhouse bedroom. A tickle on her chin woke her up. Her **dachshund** and best friend, **Calamity Jane,** was standing on her chest, licking her face. "Oh Calamity, it can't already be morning!"

Wendy Jo gazed longingly across the room, at the pictures of her favorite singers and movie stars. A loud *voice* suddenly shook Wendy Jo out of her sleepy daydreaming. "Wendy Jo! It's time to wake up, get dressed, do your chores, and get to school!" her father's booming voice announced. "And another thing… why are you sleeping in your cowboy boots again?"

2

When Wendy Jo rolled over and looked down at the floor, she saw the haunting shadows and shoes, of both her parents standing in the doorway. Wendy Jo sighed and said to herself, "Why are my parents so weird? I wish they could understand me, and that I *love* wearing cowboy boots."

Wendy Jo groaned, "Ugh! I don't want to go to school."

"Why not? Is there a problem?" asked her mother, who was still halfway hidden in the shadows. "If you don't go to school, there's no playing, singing, or artwork today!"

"Uh, well… my stomach hurts," Wendy Jo moaned.

"Haven't we been over this a hundred times? No more excuses, Wendy Jo. You *have* to go to school!" her father said sternly.

After getting dressed for school and putting on her makeshift crayon holder and microphone holster, Wendy Jo trudged into the kitchen to get a bowl of cereal. Still half asleep, she started pouring her favorite cereal into her bowl. Out came too many Golden Nugget Pops, and with a KERPLUNK, a bright yellow magnifying glass fell out. Along with it, even more golden bits spilled over onto the table and floor. Calamity was more than happy to help clean it up, quickly wolfing it down. Wendy Jo picked up the prize and happily decided that her day might not be so bad after all. "I can't believe it! I just won my very own *Imagicadabra*!"

Imagicadabra in hand, Wendy Jo grabbed her bowl of cereal and headed into the living room. Plopping down in front of the TV, she took a bite and watched her favorite show, *Vippi Mouse*. While peering at the TV screen through her toy Imagicadabra, she was startled to see a gigantic, magnified eyeball staring back at her.

"Are you okay, Wendy Jo? You look so sad," came the voice of the large brown and yellow mouse, who was looking through his own Imagicadabra.

Wendy Jo gasped, almost choking on her breakfast, and blurted out, "Hey, you're talking to ME! So you must know me from the letter I sent!"

"Yes, of course! But I've always known you, Wendy Jo! Remember, I am Vippi Mouse, the VIP *Private Investigator* and Treasure Hunting *Navigator*. I'm also the world's foremost *Expert-Expert Vippiologist*, on the most valuable treasures in the universe, including everything *V.I.P. – Very Important People, Places, and Powers.* You know, very important people like the *Fromager*, who is the maker of my favorite *nuggets* of golden cheese curds. But especially VIP's like you, Wendy Jo!"

"Hey, wait a minute. How are you talking to me through the TV?"

"Well, simply put, I have the original Imagicadabra that allows me to communicate with the one in your hand. I'll tell you more about that later. Right now, I'd like to talk to you about that *Vippigram* letter you wrote to me, last week**.**"

Vippi Mouse gazed through his Imagicadabra and muttered, "Now, where is that letter? It has to be in one of these trunks," he said hurriedly as he tossed objects from the trunks, over his shoulder.

Wendy Jo was both amused and embarrassed about the fuss, as she watched the distracted mouse make a mess, *rummaging* through the old trunk. Pirate treasure maps, gem stones, gold nuggets, an ancient book, brass cymbals, a trumpet, and even a Viking helmet sailed across the TV screen. He came upon a tempting wedge of cheese, which Vippi sniffed and placed on the side of the chest for later.

After a few minutes of digging around in the old trunk, Vippi found the letter he was searching for. Holding it in his paw, he proudly exclaimed, "Aha! I knew it had to be in there somewhere," and then he began to read aloud.

Dear Vippi,

*I feel sad because I just started going to a new school, and some of the kids there make fun of me because I have red hair, freckles, like to sing, and wear cowboy boots. They say I look like a boy. I feel like I don't belong, and I'm never part of their group. It makes me feel like nobody likes me, and that I don't matter or fit in. I don't feel at **home** there, so I've decided that I never, ever want to go back to school or even try to make friends again! I wish there was something else I could do. Can you help me?*

Sincerely,
Wendy Jo

Vippi tilted his head, looked at Wendy Jo and said, "Wendy Jo, sadly some people **F.E.A.R.** (*False Evidence Appearing Real)*, which is another kind of *fear*, things and people that are different."

"They are afraid of me?"

"They judged you before they knew you, and that's called *prejudice*."

"But why were they mean?"

Vippi explained, "Prejudice can lead to **hatred**, **stereotyping**, and **labeling** of others. The cure for **hate** and F.E.A.R., is love and **knowledge**. Don't let their words take up space in your head and make you feel bad about yourself! **Remember, you *do* matter and belong! You are a very treasured, loved, and important person with unique traits and gifts that are more valuable than *gold*.** Besides Wendy Jo, the *Treasure Chest of Life*, or what I call *TCL*, would be a boring place if you were just like everyone else. In *Vippi Code* that's the treasure of *diversity*. So, *respecting* each other's differences is a very important power!"

Wendy Jo jumped up with her hands on her hips and roared, "That's easy for you to say. You don't have red hair, freckles, or wear cowboy boots!"

"Try going through life looking like a mouse with a fat belly, whiskers, and brown and yellow fur," Vippi replied. "In case you haven't noticed, I wear cowboy boots sometimes, and I happen to like your red hair and freckles! I bet if we put our *Thinkin' Caps* on, we could solve this problem together!"

"How are we going to do that?" Wendy Jo asked.

Vippi twirled his magnifying glass around, and whispered, "It's not called an Imagicadabra for nothing!"

10

Vippi waved his paw in a circle over the Imagicadabra, and chanted these mysterious, *magical words*;

"Secret treasure, secret code, in a song from days of old. If you know the secret key, you will live in harmony."

Inside the glass, a mist started swirling and spiraling. Then sparkles of gold light and music notes began shooting out of the Imagicadabra and the TV! Wendy Jo didn't know what would happen next, so she grabbed Calamity, and backed away from the TV.

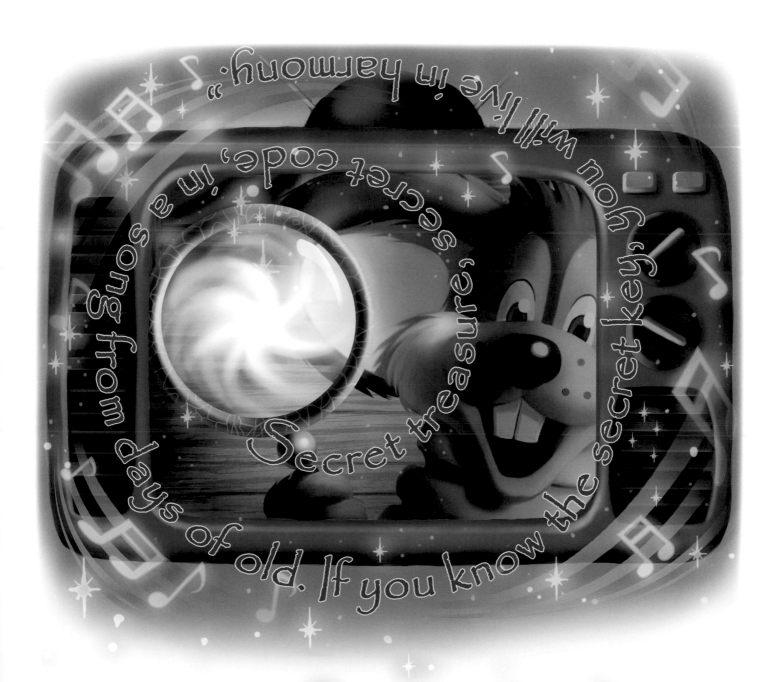

There was a crackle in the air followed by a WHOOSH and a BANG. Then there was a twinkling of gold dust, and a breeze of music in the air, as Wendy Jo and Calamity's hats blew right off their heads. Wendy Jo couldn't believe her eyes when Vippi materialized right in front of them. He coughed and brushed the gold dust off of Calamity's twitching nose.

As the gold dust settled, Calamity started wagging her tail. Wendy Jo could see that Vippi was carrying a small treasure chest under his arm.

Vippi extended his paw to Wendy Jo and greeted her kindly, "Nice to finally meet you, Wendy Jo!"

She shook his furry paw and replied, "It's nice to meet you too, Vippi Mouse!"

2 — BEING BULLIED

Vippi asked, "Now that we've met each other, perhaps you might tell me more about your problem?"

"Ugh," Wendy Jo groaned. "It makes my stomach feel sick to think about it, much less talk about it."

"Happens to me when I eat too much cheese," Vippi said, trying to cheer her up. "Even if it's difficult, talking about it, will help. I promise!"

"Well, there's a group of kids at my new school that laugh at me and say rude things about my red hair and freckles. They even grab my cowboy hat off of my head and say that I look like a boy. To make it even worse, they've started calling me "Wild West Wendy Jo." That's how I got the nickname. I thought those kids were my friends, but friends don't make fun of you, or make you feel bad and sad. That's why I'm never going to school ever again!"

"That's about as rotten as a moldy cheese problem. Nobody deserves to be **bullied**. Your story reminds me of the infamous **Claimjumper Pakk Ratts** that I once had to deal with! In Vippi Code, Claimjumpers are **varmints** that try to claim space that isn't theirs, and they'll even try to take up valuable space in your head, if you let them." Vippi knew how it felt and asked her, "Have you talked about it with your parents, teachers or school principal yet?"

"No Way! The kids will think I'm a tattletale or snitch and things might even get worse!" Wendy Jo said in a voice full of tears.

Vippi held up his paw, "Now that is a big problem! Have you come up with any better **solutions** than not going to school?"

14

Wendy Jo thought for a minute and said with disappointment, "I don't think there's anything else that I can do about it."

"Sure there is! There's always a solution. Oh, I have an idea. Let's go back in time and look at what happened yesterday," Vippi suggested.

"How are we going to do that?"

"With my Imagicadabra, of course!" Once again Vippi started chanting the **magic** words. *"Secret treasure, secret code, in a song from days of old, if you know the secret key, you will live in harmony."*

He held the magnifying glass so they could both look into it. Finally, through the misty glass they were able to see a sad Wendy Jo sitting on the school playground. Wendy Jo sighed, and with a tear rolling down her cheek, began to watch.

15

3 — IMAGINATIONS

Vippi gazed at her with a concerned look on his face. "So this is where it all started, eh?" he asked Wendy Jo. Tears had welled up so big in her eyes that she could barely see. "May I make a suggestion before we begin? Instead of reliving the moment in such a painful way, why don't we use our *imaginations* so we can make it a little less hurtful?"

Wiping away the tears, Wendy Jo finally felt a glimmer of hope. She asked, "How do we do that?"

"That's **Easy-Cheesy**! Let's *imagine* it from the perspective of your beloved cowboy boots!" Vippi said.

16

"Let's take a look at what happened!"

Together they watched as a pair of bullies, or rather ***Powerless Ugly –
P.U. Shoes***, walked towards Wendy Jo, or rather her cowboy boots. When
the P.U. Shoes were a few feet away from her, they pointed at Wendy Jo,
laughed, and called her names. Wendy Jo was *shakin'* in her boots, when
suddenly there was a whole gang of odd-looking shoes surrounding her,
all of them being unkind. One pair even tried to take her cherished cowboy
hat. To make matters worse, there was another group of **bystander** shoes
just standing around watching the **bullying** and they didn't do anything
about it. In fact, some of them even laughed and whispered. That seemed to
encourage the shoes who were being unkind to be even more unkind!

Vippi shook his head in disappointment and consoled Wendy, "I'm sorry
that happened to you! They have what I call ***Stinkin' Thinkin'*** and ***Herd
Behavior***!" Vippi tried to cheer her up with a little humor, "Nothing's
worse than a ***soleless*** herd of shoes that aren't thinkin' for themselves.
Keep your distance from P.U. Shoes! ***Don't Touch, Don't Wear, Don't
Smell, Don't Care!*** It's a ***choice*** of negative thinking, and in Vippi Code,
Stinkin' Thinkin's not OK! Nobody deserves to be treated that way!"

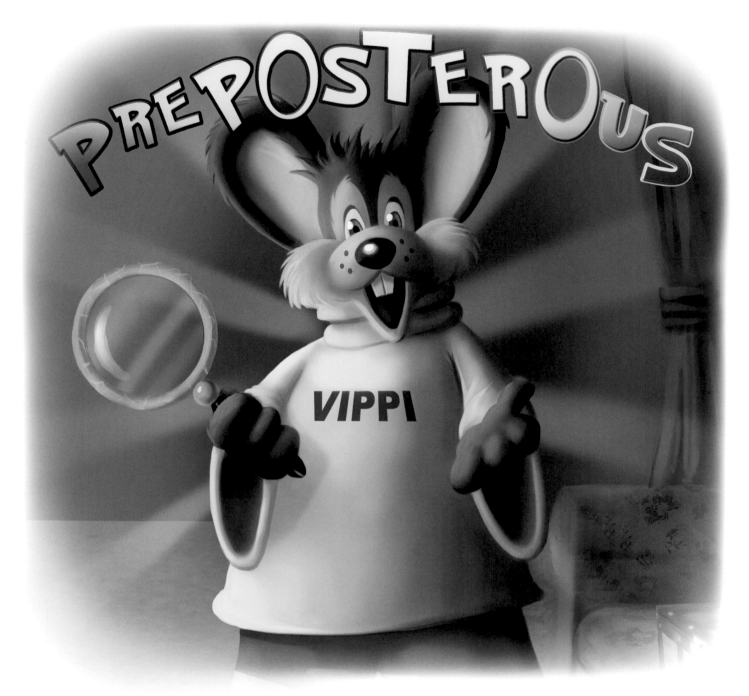

"It makes me feel like I don't matter and that I'm all alone. It's just not fair, and I feel powerless to do anything about it," Wendy Jo added.

Seeing Wendy Jo in so much pain really struck a chord with Vippi and he shouted, "That's **PREPOSTEROUS**! Of course you matter, Wendy Jo! Don't let those darn Claimjumpers take up space in your head! Life isn't always fair, but you know what? You can be *A-OK Anyway*, because YOU are a very important person with a very important power!"

Wendy Jo shrugged her shoulders in disbelief, "What power could I possibly have?"

4 — A VERY IMPORTANT POWER

Vippi reached into the treasure chest and pulled out a glowing *golden nugget of wisdom*, with the word *CHOICE* written on it, and held it up proudly. "See this choice nugget? This is a powerful nugget of gold like the kind found on *bedrock,* that a *prospector*, might call a *picker*, unlike *Fool's Gold* which has no power," Vippi said with a wink and grin.

"Seriously though, everyone has the very important power of choice, which is to choose, pick, or decide. Here are the two different types of choices we make:

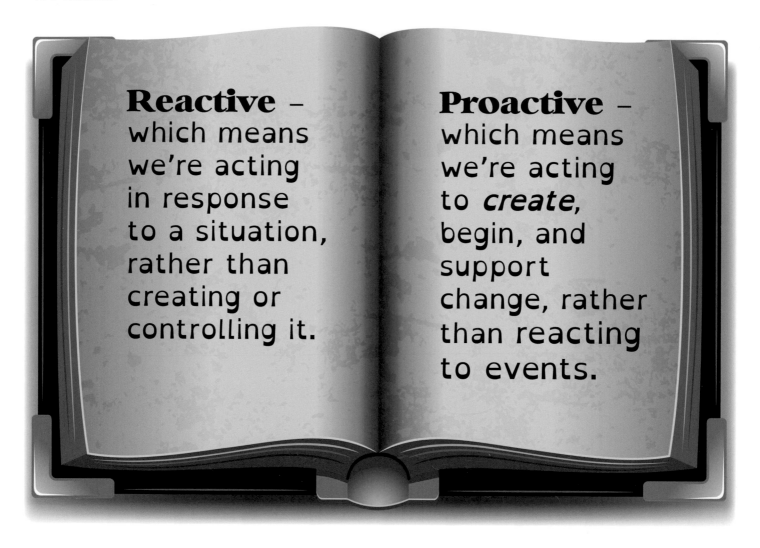

Reactive – which means we're acting in response to a situation, rather than creating or controlling it.

Proactive – which means we're acting to *create*, begin, and support change, rather than reacting to events.

Vippi summed it up like the Expert-Expert he was by declaring, "You see, you only have control over two things and you control them from under your Thinkin' Cap:

1) The thoughts you imagine and think

2) The reactive and proactive choices you make—which are the actions and behavior you choose. 'Different problems call for different solutions and choices, and there's ***Always a Solution***!'"

21

"Using the very important power of choice, what do you think could be the best solution to your problem?" Vippi asked.

"Well, since I've already decided that I'm NOT going to school. I guess that's not a problem I have to deal with anymore!" Wendy Jo defiantly proclaimed.

Vippi thought for a minute and asked, "Do you think not going to school will fix the problem in the long run?"

Wendy Jo looked up to the ceiling

as if searching for an answer. "It doesn't feel like a permanent solution, because I know that eventually I will have to go back to school. My parents will make me. And I love learning and making friends!"

"Now that's **Cool Thinkin'**! In **Vippi Code**, it means positive or good thinking!" Vippi cheered.

Vippi pulled his cheesy cowboy hat out of the treasure chest, and put it on his head. That reminded Wendy Jo and Calamity to find their hats, too.

 "Now that we all have our Thinkin' Caps on, can you imagine some powerful choices that might help make this situation better?"

Wendy Jo thought for a second and then answered. "I could walk away and remove myself from the situation."

"As well as use the power of your *voice*." Vippi reminded her.

That gave Wendy Jo an idea. "Yes! *I Have A Choice – The Power Of Voice! I could stand up and say, 'Hey! That's Not Okay! It's Stinkin' Thinkin'!'* I could also choose to just ignore their words and not react at all," Wendy Jo exclaimed.

"*Eureka*! Those are powerful choices."

"I would even call them golden nuggets of wisdom straight from the TCL – Treasure Chest of Life," Vippi exclaimed with joy. "Can you think of anything else?" the Expert-Expert asked.

"I should probably tell my parents what's bothering me," Wendy Jo blurted out. Then a serious look came across her face and she said, "Maybe I could tell my teacher or even go straight to the school principal."

"Now you're Thinkin' like an Expert-Expert, Wendy Jo! Yes, trusted adults and **upstanders**, can help guide everyone involved to make better choices and feel safer. Those are all excellent examples of owning your power and standing up for yourself when you are being bullied!"

5 — BYSTANDERS

"Now let's look back through the Imagicadabra at the bystanders. Can you see how the bystanders are standing around watching the bullying take place? Let's imagine if you were in the bystander shoes. Can you think of some other choices besides just standing there?"

Wendy Jo thought and thought about Vippi's question. "I am not sure yet what choices I would make, but I know some that I would NOT make! I would not join in laughing or doing anything that would encourage the ones who are being unkind! That would give them power, and I'd be giving my own power away," the feisty cowboy boot-wearing, redhead declared.

"If I were in their shoes, I would choose to be an upstander and *leader* instead of a bystander, and if it were safe, I would stand up for the person being bullied."

Wendy Jo, thoughtfully continued, "No matter what, I'd be a good friend and ask them to walk with me to a safer place."

"Wendy Jo, those are *excellent choices* and examples of what I call Cool Thinkin'. In Vippi Code, that's *positive thinkin'*! When you imagine walking in someone else's shoes, you can see how they might feel. That's what you call *empathy* and *compassion*." Vippi continued. "That reminds me, have you ever heard of *The Compass of Cool*?"

"What's that?" Wendy Jo asked.

26

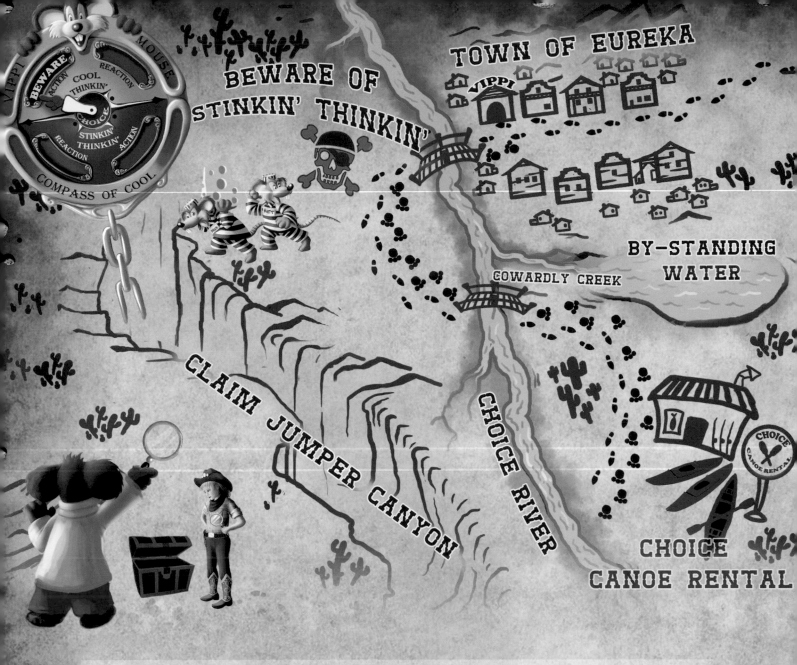

"Well, let me show you. A **compass** is a **navigation** instrument used by navigators and treasure hunters to find their way. There are many types of compasses, but my favorite is the **inner compass**, which is where your head consults your heart and gut for the best outcome. As a VIP Investigator and Treasure Hunting Navigator, I use a compass and maps to point me in the right direction whenever I'm not sure which choice or road to take. It helps me beware of Stinkin' Thinkin', especially when dealing with P.U. Shoes, Claimjumper Ratts, or bullies. That way I don't get lost."

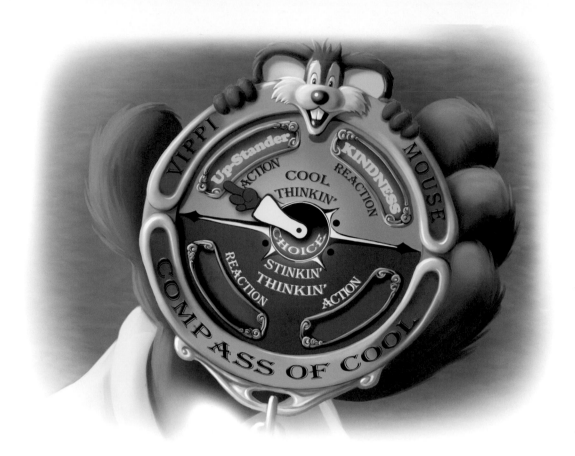

Vippi then reached in his treasure chest and pulled out a large, shiny, yellow and blue compass. "The Compass of Cool is my invention, which is based on the **Golden Rule**. In Vippi Code, it stands for: ***Be cool AND rule, with the best KIND of power***! Right now the compass is pointing in the direction of the word *kindness*, which means, always treat people the way you'd like to be treated."

"I wish I were cool!" Wendy Jo said.

"You are cool AND rule, Wendy Jo! By choosing to follow the Compass of Cool and making the choice to have empathy and be an upstander, you have chosen to use your own power to make a positive difference and to change the world for the better! That's the best kind of power, and makes you especially cool!"

"Well, what about people who choose to **bully** others? Aren't they trying to be cool, too?" Wendy Jo pondered.

"Sometimes people think that they're being powerful and cool when they bully others, but that's not cool at all! Not only is that kind of behavior *uncool*, it's *cowardly* and *unacceptable*!"

28

6 - BULLYING

"Now that we have the Compass of Cool as our guide, let's look through the Imagicadabra at the one who is doing the bullying. What choices might you make if you were walking in the bully's shoes?"

Wendy Jo thought for a moment. "If I were the one walking in the bully's shoes, I would first want to put my Thinkin' Cap on to consider my choices. I would ask myself – is this Cool Thinkin' or Stinkin' Thinkin'? Then I would ask myself, if my choices would be worth it in the long run. Being unkind is not only hurtful, but people might treat *me* poorly also. They might even be scared and just **pretend** to be my friend, so I wouldn't bully them too. Then I wouldn't have the treasure of true **friendship**!"

"They also wouldn't want to share their cheese with you!" Vippi blurted out with a squeak. "There's a price to be paid in the long run, when you hurt others. When you're unkind to someone else, it hurts you as much as the other person!"

"Can you imagine some better choices for the ones doing the bullying?"

"If I were in their shoes, I would find an upstanding adult who could help me find healthier ways to deal with my feelings, rather than being a bully. I could also try to respect myself and others by following the Compass of Cool. Being an upstander is where the real power is!" answered Wendy Jo, excitedly.

"Hey! That's A-OK Cool Thinkin', and great choices!" Vippi cheered as he high-fived Wendy Jo. "Cruel words are like moldy globs of cheese. They look, smell, and taste terrible. Not even Claimjumper Ratts want to mess with them. Choosing to live by the Compass of Cool, being **considerate** of others, and thinking about the **consequences** of your actions, is a big step towards living a life that is filled with treasures more precious than gold."

"So, Wendy Jo, would you like to try out your own Imagicadabra and test your powers?" Vippi asked.

Wendy Jo's eyes opened wide, looking at her cereal box prize, she squealed, "You mean I could do the same thing with my own Imagicadabra?"

"Well, of course you can, Wendy Jo. Let's give it a try!" Vippi whispered.

7 - MAGIC AND SECRET POWERS

Vippi handed Wendy Jo the compass, and reassured her. "Go ahead, Wendy Jo. Choose your destination from the Compass of Cool. Then look into your Imagicadabra, say the magic words, and imagine your wish fulfilled. Your imagination is so powerful, that you can see back in time, and into the future. Let's take a look!" Vippi happily announced.

Wendy Jo excitedly held her Imagicadabra and the Compass of Cool, and started to chant the "*Secret Treasure, Secret Code…*" Coming into view was the bullying that she had experienced the other day.

As she watched the playground scene and relived what happened, Wendy Jo felt sad. Then she remembered Vippi's motto, "***You Have a Choice – The Power of Voice".*** Suddenly, the Compass of Cool dial shot up to the mark of Cool Thinkin' and ***courage***, and in a ***hero's*** instant, Wendy Jo chose to be brave and use her voice to speak up. She grabbed her microphone out of her holster, looked them in the eye and said, "Hey! That's Not OK, and besides, it's Stinkin' Thinkin'! I'll have you know, I like my red hair!" When Wendy Jo made the choice to own and use her power and show confidence, the unkind shoes didn't know what else to say, and they gave up.

8 — UPSTANDERS

What happened next was just short of a miracle! As they continued to watch, suddenly from out of nowhere, a **courageous** pair of bystander shoes made the powerful choice of Cool Thinkin', to become upstanders for kindness and **inclusion**. As they smiled and walked towards Wendy Jo, one of them asked, "Hey, are you okay?"

Wendy Jo did a **thumbs up** and said, "Yes! I'm A-Ok!" After seeing **social proof**, several other pairs of bystander shoes chose to be upstanders as well. When the shoes that were being unkind and did the bullying, saw how it felt to be excluded, they decided that they wanted to be cool and included, instead. The reward for becoming an upstander and being kind, resulted in finding the treasure of new-found friendships for all.

"So, you see, Wendy Jo, genuine power is first found by choosing to follow your heart and your inner compass, and then using the Compass of Cool as a reminder and guide." Vippi smiled and asked, "Do you feel the power of your choices?"

34

"Yes, I feel powerful because I made the choice to use my voice and be an upstander! Now I'm looking forward to going back to school, so I can try out what I've learned. I can't wait to tell my parents!"

"EUREKA!" Vippi Mouse cheered, "YOU are an Expert-Expert now!

"Wendy Jo, before I go I want to present you with an ***Expert-Expert Badge.***" Vippi pulled the shiny gold star from the treasure chest and said, "Please wear this as a reminder that whenever you have a problem, you can use your inner compass and Cool Thinkin' to make the right choices. In other words, Be *Cool* and *Rule*, with the best **KIND** of *Power*!"

Wendy Jo thanked him, and proudly pinned it on her favorite cowgirl shirt. The big yellow mouse extended a paw and said, "Congratulations, Wendy Jo! You are now officially what I call, an Expert-Expert Vippiologist and ***Treasure Hunter***!"

Vippi put both paws in the air and cheered. "Now let's celebrate with the ***Vippi Dance***!" He then looked over at the TV and said, "Hit it!" His favorite song – ***You Have the Power***, filled the air. Vippi, Wendy Jo, and Calamity, high-fived each other as they danced like a rowdy bunch of prospectors who had just struck gold!

Wendy Jo yelled above the music. "Hey! Vippi! Now I see why you chose to study Vippiology and become a VIP Investigator and Treasure Hunting Navigator!"

"That's right!" Vippi proclaimed. ***"My quest is to inspire people to discover the most valuable treasures in the universe, like THEMSELVES, The treasure that is greater than gold!"***

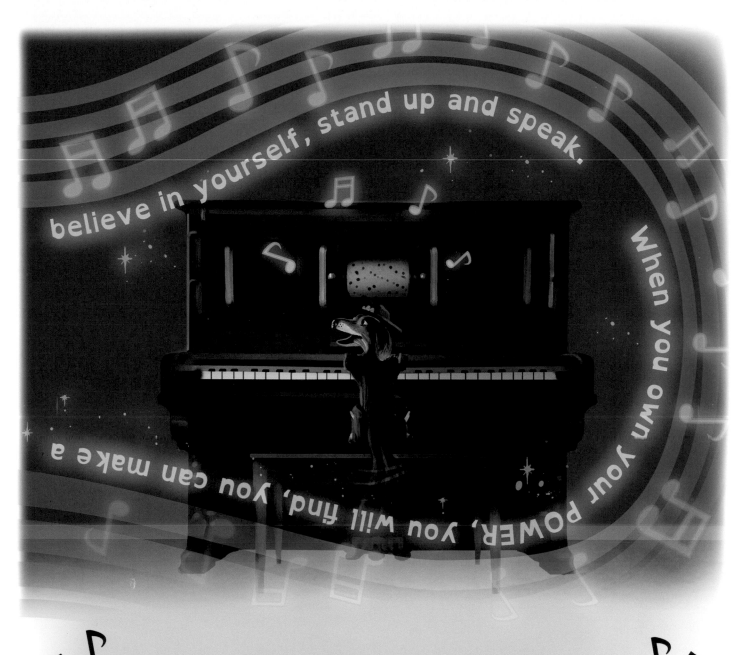

"You have the power! You have the key! Believe in yourself, stand up and speak! When you own your power, you will find, you can make a difference, when you are kind. Anytime someone's feeling down, help lift them up, wipe off that frown. We all feel that way once in a while. Just pick yourself up and go the extra mile! Can you feel it, feel the power? It's a state of mind. Feel it. Feel the power, when we treat others kind."

The song was almost over when Vippi noticed the time and said, "Yikes! Where did all the time go? I had better find my way back to the TV before this *Vippi Treasure Quest Show* is over!"

"Wait, don't leave! Where are you going?" asked a concerned Wendy Jo.

Vippi reassured her and said, "Don't worry! It's time to say goodbye now, but just for today."

With that, Vippi gazed into his Imagicadabra and chanted the magic words, "*Secret Treasure, Secret Code…*"

9 — BACK TO THE PRESENT

In the blink of an eye, Vippi was right back where he started on the Vippi Treasure Quest Show stage, with his grown-up pal, Wild West Wendy Jo.

Astonished, Wendy Jo exclaimed, "Wow! Vippi, that was quite a trip down memory lane, seeing my childhood through the Imagicadabra! It was almost as if we were actually there, instead of here on our TV show."

Wendy Jo looked down and saw something shiny. "Hey, how did my Expert-Expert badge get on my shirt? I thought I lost that years ago!"

With a wink and a grin, Vippi Mouse clued her in, **"*You never know what you'll find when you travel back in time…*"**

"Vippi, I want to thank you for helping me when I felt powerless and alone as a young 'un. You helped me to discover the real power of my voice, and I learned that I've always had the choice to feel good about myself no matter what others say or do! I'm happy that both of us can help today's kids navigate issues like bullying, and the new problem of ***cyberbullying***. My motto is; "***Help Kids Be Safe, in the Wild West of Cyberspace!***" I'm also excited to have the opportunity to show my ***gratitude***, and ***pay it forward*** by helping you guide young people on their own treasure quest ***expeditions.*** They'll discover the most valuable treasures in the Universe, such as friendship, kindness, courage, and *themselves,* the treasure that is greater than gold."

Wendy Jo yawned and stretched, "Vippi, I feel like we've been ***traveling*** for years. It's time for me to head home now."

Vippi chuckled as he pointed at his own head, "Wendy Jo, you're ALREADY home because ***Home Is Where You Hang Your Thinkin' Cap!*** In Vippi Code, that means you have the power of choice to feel at home wherever you are."

Vippi and Wild West Wendy Jo, turned, waved at the audience, and said, "See ya' next time!"

"THAT'S SO EASY, IT'S ALMOST CHEESY!"

Our next treasure quest awaits...

VIPPIOLOGY CODE GLOSSARY

A-OK Anyway™:
A very important power of choice, to feel okay and good about yourself, no matter what others say and do. To feel at home and comfortable in your own skin and your own head. Example; *"Hey are you OK? Yes! I'm A-OK"!* (See choice, Thinkin' Cap, Cool Thinkin', home, Positive Thinkin', power, proactive, Very Important Power, You Have The Power, and voice)

Action:
An act of will or cause. Making a choice, or doing something which will create and produce a reaction. (See proactive, reactive, reaction, choice, and Thinkin' Cap)

Bedrock:
A solid rock bottom, where gold and treasures can often be found. Also refers to a base or foundation. *"When you hit rock bottom, remember, bedrock is where you find the gold!"™* – Wild West Wendy Jo (See gold, picker, nugget)

Bully / Bullies / Bullying/ Bullied:
When someone with PU Stinkin' Thinkin' tries to take or claim your space and power through fear and/or intimidation. Often, the bully has fear and insecurities, which motivates them to bully others. (See power, P.U. Shoe, F.E.A.R., Claimjumpers and varmint)

Bystander:
Someone who gives up their power or chance to help someone else, by being unconcerned or unsure of what to do. They sometimes wait to see what others are going to do, and then follow or imitate them, without thinking for themselves, or of the consequences. (See uncool, power, Thinkin' Cap, Stinkin' Thinkin', social proof, herd behavior, and upstander)

Calamity aka Calamity Jane:
Ruckus, rumble, rumpus, messy, hullabaloo, comedian. In short, a brave, free spirited, toothless wiener dog named after a famous cowgirl Calamity Jane. (See dachshund)

Choice:
A Very Important Power and ability to decide, choose, or pick from two or more options that will create a reaction or consequence. (See power, proactive, reactive, picker, action, reaction, and decide)

Claimjumper Pakk Ratts™:
An uncool, Stinkin' Thinkin' pack of varmints, ClaimJumpers, or bullies, that sometimes travel in packs (gangs), to overpower a person or animal that appears vulnerable, alone, and/or scared, or to claim a place or thing that isn't theirs. They try to claim territory, space and pack away, anything of power and value that isn't theirs. They'll even try to claim your power, and take up valuable space in your head, if you let them. (See power, bully, varmint, Stinkin' Thinkin, cowardly, uncool, prospector, and F.E.A.R.)

Compass / Compass of Cool™:
A navigation tool, to help navigators like Vippi Mouse, and treasure hunters, find the right direction, so they don't get lost. Vippi's Compass of Cool, is based on the golden rule. *"Be Cool AND Rule, With The Best Kind Of Power!"™*. Unlike a magnetic compass, it is able to assist your inner compass to find the right direction in order to make powerful, wise and cool choices that will lead to the greatest treasures in the universe. (See inner compass, TCL, excellent choices, The Golden Rule, Golden Cool, choice, power, cool, uncool, reactive, and proactive)

Compassion:
A Very Important Power and ability to imagine walking in someone else's shoes, and to sympathize with how they might feel. (See empathy, power, choice, heart, upstander, and Cool Thinkin')

Consequences:
The results of an action or choice. (See action, choice, reactive, proactive, result and reaction)

Considerate:
Using your Thinkin' Cap and Compass Of Cool, to make excellent choices and show careful thought not to inconvenience or hurt others. (Thinkin' Cap, Cool Thinkin', kindness, upstander, excellent choices, Compass Of Cool, inner compass, heart, love, respect, and Golden Cool)

Cool:
Very good, excellent, and smart. Also, fashionable and hip. A cool person, who is an Expert-Expert and owns their power, makes good choices, and has a cool head and attitude. (See Kindness, Compass Of Cool, Expert-Expert, Cool Thinkin', upstander, hero, considerate, and courage)

Cool Thinkin'™:
Proactive and positive thinking. Optimistic and constructive thinking that is problem solving and solution oriented. (See cool, Stinkin' Thinkin', Positive Thinkin', Thinkin' Cap, Compass Of Cool, Code Of Ethics, and upstander)

Courage / Courageous:

The ability to be brave and do something that scares one, and to face fear. Upstanders, heroes, and Expert-Experts, have courage and bravery. (See fear, F.E.A.R., upstander, hero, Cool Thinkin', Expert-Expert, inner compass, and Compass of Cool)

Create:

A Very Important Power of bringing something into existence. To cause something to happen as a result of one's choices, imagination, and/or actions. To produce, generate, bring into being, make, fabricate, fashion, build, construct. (See choice, imagine, power, TCL, proactive, and VIP)

Cyberbullying:

The cowardly and uncool act of bullying someone through electronic means. Sometimes done directly, or anonymously, by texting or posting mean or threatening messages online, to or about someone. *"Help Kids Be Safe, in the Wild West of Cyberspace!"*™ – Wild West Wendy Jo (See cyberspace, Stinkin' Thinkin', uncool, P.U. Shoe, bullying, F.E.A.R. hate, herd behavior, Claimjumper Pakk Ratts, power, and unacceptable)

Cyberspace:

The internet and online web of computer networks, connecting the world. (See cyberbullying)

Dachshund:

A brave, feisty, small breed of dog, with short legs and a long, powerful body. It's often referred to as a wiener dog because of its shape, and funny personality. This is Wild West Wendy Jo's favorite breed of dog. (See Calamity)

Decide:

A Very Important Power. To be proactive and make up one's mind by making a definite choice and decision, which will set creation, action, and reaction in motion. (See create, choice, proactive, action, result, imagine, and reaction)

Diversity:

One of the most valuable treasures in the universe is the vast and different varieties and differences of people, cultures, and things in the universe. It enhances society and the depth of human experience. Respecting each other's differences is A Very Important Power. *"Variety is the spice of life"*. (See TCL, treasure, respect, considerate, power, and love)

Easy-Cheesy™:

Vippi's favorite kind of choice (in addition to cheese), is a gold nugget solution to a problem. A choice that might not be the easiest to make, but it's easy to see in the long run, the positive results make life grand and full of TCL treasures. (See nugget, choice, proactive, and TCL)

Empathy / Empathetic:

A Very Important Power and ability to *imagine walking in someone else's shoes*, and sharing understanding of how they might feel. (See choice, heart, compassion, upstander, and considerate)

Eureka:

A prospector's cry of joy or satisfaction when they find or discover gold and treasures. Can also be a place name.

Excellent Choices:

Cool choices that Expert-Expert Vippiologists make, using their Cool Thinkin' Cap, inner compass, heart, and Compass Of Cool. Choices that usually solve problems and result in the best outcome. (See Cool Thinkin', Expert-Expert, power, Very Important Power, Compass Of Cool, inner compass, and upstander)

Expedition:

A treasure quest, journey or voyage embarked on by a group of Vippiologists, and people looking for something in particular, like a treasure, or scientific research and exploration.

Expert-Expert™ / Expert-Expert Code of Ethics™, Expert-Expert Badge™:

The Vippiology code of ethics and badge which stands for the best of the best in skills, values, and being ethical and honorable in all things, including treasure hunting and Vippiology. Expert-Experts are knowledgeable, experienced and wise. (See Vippi Mouse, Wild West Wendy Jo, fromager, excellent choices, hero, Golden Cool, leaders, power, treasure hunter, upstander, kindness, considerate, empathy, compassion, love, respect, Very Important Power, VIP, and Vippiologist)

Fear:

Everyone experiences fear, and it's important to know the difference between the two kinds of fear. Real fear can save your life, and imagined F.E.A.R, is like a Claimjumper Ratt, and keep you from achieving your goals and dreams. Genuine fear is a reaction and strong emotion that originates in your Thinkin' Cap by sensing, seeing, or worrying about something unknown, painful, or knowingly dangerous. It can also originate in our Thinkin' Cap, and gut, and should be listened to in order to keep you out of real danger. (See F.E.A.R., choice, inner compass, and Compass Of Cool).

F.E.A.R.:

"False Evidence Appearing Real" Everyone experiences this kind of fear sometimes, but this kind of fear is imagined. Most of the time, it is a choice of Stinkin' Thinkin' imagining and worrying about things that aren't a real threat, or that we can't do anything about. The cure and solution to F.E.A.R. is to *"Feel The Fear, And Do It Anyway!"* — Susan Jeffers. (See Stinkin' Thinkin', Thinkin' Cap, fool's gold, imagination, choice, herd behavior, prejudice, hate, labeling, bullying, P.U. Shoe, and varmint)

Fool's Gold:

Some thing or choice that looks like treasure that is not at all valuable. Iron or copper pyrite is sometimes called fool's gold, because it is mistaken for real gold. (See uncool. Stinkin' Thinkin', prejudice, P.U. Shoe, F.E.A.R., and choice)

Friend / Friendship:

A mutual relationship of trust, respect, honesty and kindness.

(See kindness, love, upstander, treasure, TCL, Vippi Mouse, Wild West Wendy Jo, dachshund, and VIP)

Gold:
One of the finest and most valuable treasures in the universe. Metaphorically, it is the symbol of the standard in value, genuine, power and pure goodness. "*Good As Gold*". In gold's mineral form, it is a rare yellow, malleable, and metallic element that was created by the collision of neutron stars, and thought to have been delivered to earth later, by asteroid impacts. Valued for use in jewelry and decoration, and to guarantee the value of currencies (money). (See love, Compass Of Cool, Golden Cool, fool's gold, eureka, TCL, prospector, and power)

Golden Cool Rule™ aka Golden Rule:
Treat others how you want to be treated. Based on the Golden Rule, but not actually a rule. It's a powerful guide to making cool and excellent choices and actions, which help you to achieve and enjoy good outcomes. (See Compass Of Cool, cool, Cool Thinkin', upstander, leader, inner compass, leader, power, solution, Very Important Powers, and TCL treasure)

Gratitude:
The Very Important Power and feeling of being thankful, and having a readiness to show appreciation and kindness in return, or by paying it forward to someone else.(See paying It Forward, Very Important Power, Power, kindness, and TCL treasure)

Hate / Hater / Hatred:
A choice derived from Stinkin' Thinkin'. An intense and emotional feeling of dislike, resentment, and aversion towards a thing, person, or group, deriving from fear, anger, or sense of injury. (See Fear, F.E.A.R., choice, Stinkin' Thinkin', bullying, prejudice, P.U. Shoe, ClaimJumper Ratt Pakk, fool's gold, and unacceptable)

Herd Behavior:
Large numbers of people or animals in a group, copying and acting in the same way at the same time. The behavior of humans and animals in herds, packs, bird flocks, fish schools, and in this story – a herd of shoes not thinking for themselves. (See fear, F.E.A.R., Thinkin' Cap, and social proof)

Hero:
A person who is admired for courage, noble qualities, brave achievements, facing fear, and who stands up for others and what is right. (See upstander, kindness, considerate, empathy, courage, and TCL).

Home:
"*Home Is Where You Hang Your Thinkin' Cap*"™. In Vippi Code that means that you have the power of choice in your own head (Thinkin' Cap), to feel comfortable in your own skin or anywhere else you may choose to belong. It's a place of being, where you feel comfortable and have a sense of belonging. (See Thinkin' Cap, *Positive* Thinkin', Cool Thinkin',TCL, power, inner compass, heart, and choice)

Imagicadabra™:
A powerful and magical time-traveling magnifying glass, invented by Vippi Mouse that is powered by your imagination, and the magic words "You never know what you'll find, when you travel back in time…"™ (See imagine, magic words, treasure quest, time travel, choice, decide, power, Vippi Treasure Quest Show, Treasure Quests, Vippi, navigator, prospector, and investigator)

Imagine / Imagination:
A Very Important Power, and ability of your Thinkin' Cap to create and re-create new ideas and images of external objects, not yet present in your physical world. The ability to visualize, daydream and travel through time, with your mind alone, and with the help of the Imagicadabra. (See Imagicadabra, power, create, choice, decide, Thinkin' Cap, Positive Thinkin', Cool Thinkin' inner compass, time travel, quest)

Inclusion:
The Very Important Power and treasure of being included and including others. To join together, and be considerate of others, by not excluding or leaving them out. (See considerate, upstander, Cool Thinkin', cool, leader, courage, kindness, excellent choices, compassion, empathy, hero, golden rule, Golden Cool, and Golden Compass of Cool)

Inner Compass:
Your own wise guide inside of you, located under your Cool Thinkin' Cap. It's where your head consults your heart and gut, for the best results and outcome. (See Thinkin' Cap, Cool Thinkin', and Compass of Cool)

Investigator:
A person, explorer, treasure hunter, or detective who researches, studies, and investigates problems, questions, and solutions to problems. (See Private Investigator, Vippi Mouse, Vippiology, treasure hunter, and Imagicadabra)

Kindness:
A Very Important Power that is both good to give and receive. Being nice and considerate to people, and treating them with respect. "*Be Cool AND Rule, With The Best Kind Of Power!*"™ (See TCL treasure, power, considerate, compassion, love, and empathy)

Labeling / Label:
To attach a name or phrase to a person or thing, especially one that is inaccurate or restrictive. Example; Name calling. Once you assign labels to people, it's hard to see them as individuals (See stereotype, prejudice, Stinkin' Thinkin', uncool, P.U. Shoe, fool's gold, F.E.A.R., and bullying)

Leader:
Someone or something that leads. A leader is the one in charge, and/or convinces other people to follow. An Expert-Expert leader, inspires confidence in other people, and leads them to good and upstanding action. There are also leaders who are corrupt and destructive bullies, and it's important not to follow leaders like that. Examples of people who can be leaders are number one –YOU, Vippi Mouse, Wild West Wendy Jo, your parents, school principle, school teacher, and the president of your country. Examples of things that lead

are a road or compass like the Compass Of Cool, which lead to destinations or results.

Love:

In Vippi Code, love is much more than A Very Important Power – it's the greatest power and treasure in the universe! It's also a choice from your heart and inner compass. Upstanders lead by choosing love over hate and F.E.A.R. Love opens all doors, breaks down all barriers of F.E.A.R. and differences. "*Love Is The Answer*" and cure to hate and F.E.A.R., and the most valuable treasure from the TCL-Treasure Chest of Life. Kindness, respect, and consideration, are powerful ways to show love. (See heart, A Very Important Power, choice, TCL treasure, power, Cool Thinkin', kindness, gratitude, respect, and inner compass)

Magic / Magical / Magic Words:

"Secret treasure, secret code, in a song from days of old. If you know the secret key, you will live in harmony."™ An extraordinary Power or influence, to move, change or create, as if miraculously. Special words, actions, and imagination, to make something feel more believable. (See Imagicadabra, imagination, imagine, VIP, and Very Important Power)

Map:

A map is a drawing of a particular area such as a city, country, or continent, which shows its main landmarks and features. Examples of features are where X marks the spot of a treasure, gold mines, mountains, water, roads, and trails.

Navigator / Navigation:

An Expert-Expert person who directs the route or course of a treasure quest, Imagicadabra, ship, aircraft, time travel, or other form of transportation, especially by using instruments like a compass and maps. (See Vippi Mouse, Imagicadabra, treasure quests, treasure hunter, Compass Of Cool, inner compass, Expert-Expert, investigator, and explorer)

Nugget / Golden Nugget of Wisdom:

In Vippi Code – A small lump of gold called a gold nugget or picker, that can be found on bedrock. Another type of nugget is a choice treasure, of wise and valuable ideas or facts. One of Vippi's favorite types of nuggets, are golden Nuggets of cheese curds. (See picker, choice, gold, and bedrock)

Pay It Forward:

A Very Important Power and choice, to respond to a person's kindness to oneself by being kind to someone else. (See gratitude)

Picker:

A wise and cool choice. Prospector slang for a choice gold or golden nugget. (See nugget, choice, TCL, and cool).

Positive Thinkin':

The Very Important Power and choice of Cool Thinkin', and imagining the outcome of what you want and desire, instead of what you don't want. (See choice, decide, Thinkin' Cap, Cool Thinkin' vs Stinkin' Thinkin')

Power:

It's a treasure so valuable that you must guard it from Claim-jumper Pakk Ratts, bullies, and others who may want to steal it from you. It's a valuable treasure and ability that you already have access to. It is found in your Thinkin' Cap (brain), and can help you make choices, decide, and direct or influence your own and other's behavior, and the course of events. (See choice, love, Cool Thinkin', ClaimJumper Ratt Pakk, leader, upstander, and bully)

Prejudice / Prejudge:

"*You can't judge a book, by its cover.*" which means you shouldn't prejudge the worth or value of something by its outward appearance alone. Bullying, and prejudging someone or something that is different, and having an opinion about them that is not based on reason or actual experience, is often based out of fear. (See diversity, Stinkin' Thinkin', uncool, P.U. Shoe, fool's gold, F.E.A.R., and bullying)

Pretend:

Being, acting, and imagining in an unreal way, sometimes for fun, and in creating something. It's sometimes used for protection, and but can also be perceived as fake or phony. (See fool's gold and imagine)

Private Investigator / P.I.:

A freelance detective who carries out investigations into problems, crimes, and mysteries, in order to find answers, truths, and solutions. The P.I. in Vippi, stands for Private Investigator. (See Vippi)

Proactive:

Using the Very Important Power of Choice and taking action to create, begin, and support change, rather than reacting to events. (See action, Easy Cheesy, power, choice, excellent choices, create, treasure, cool, Cool Thinkin' Positive Thinkin', and Expert-Expert).

Prospector:

A prospector is a treasure hunter and explorer, who searches for things of value, including gold, nuggets of wisdom, minerals, and treasures from the TCL – Treasure Chest Of Life. When they find gold and treasure they are famous for saying "Eureka!" Prospectors use various tools depending on what kinds of treasures they are searching for. When searching for TCL treasures, they use the Imagicadabra, Compass Of Cool, their inner compass, and Thinkin' Cap. When searching for gold and minerals, they use tools such as a directional compass, gold pans, metal detectors, and shovels. (See treasure hunter, navigator, investigator, treasure quest, Expert-Expert, Picker, Vippi, and Wild West Wendy Jo)

P.U. Shoe™ / Powerless Ugly:

A stinky shoe character that represents Stinkin Thinkin' and **P**owerless **U**gly choices and behavior like bullying. Stay away from them! "*Don't Touch, Don't Wear, Don't Smell, Don't Care!*"™ (See Bully/Bullies/Bullying, Stinkin' Thinkin', Claimjumpers, fool's gold, F.E.A.R., Claimjumper Pakk Ratts, herd behavior, uncool, and varmint)

Quest / Mission Statement:

A search, pursuit, mission, or expedition to find treasures and answers to questions. *"Our quest is to inspire people to discover the most valuable treasures in the universe, like THEMSELVES. The treasure that is greater than gold!"™* (See treasure quest, explorer, prospector, and investigator)

Reactive:

A reaction or response to a situation, rather than creating or controlling it. (See choice and reaction)

Respect / Respecting / Respectful:

A very important power of being considerate of the feelings, wishes, rights, traditions, and differences of others.(See considerate, diversity, upstander, Cool Thinkin', VIP, power, love, and Golden Cool)

Result:

A consequence, effect, or outcome of something. (See reactive and reaction)

Rummaging / Rummage:

To search for something in a scattered, disorganized, and sometimes messy way.

Social Proof:

When people don't know what to do, and look for social evidence and wait to see what others are going to do, and then imitate them. When people don't use their own Thinkin' Cap to think for themselves, when faced with a choice. (See bystander, leader, herd behavior, fear, F.E.A.R., choice, decide, and Thinkin' Cap)

Soleless aka Souless:

Lacking or suggesting the lack of human feelings, qualities, character, and individuality. Shoes that don't have a sturdy sole to walk on.

Solution:

A Means of solving a problem or difficult situation. A result and reaction of Cool Thinkin' and the power of choice. (See Choice, TCL, Compass Of Cool, result, reaction, and Cool Thinkin', Thinkin' Cap, proactive, decide, quest and choice)

Stereotype/ Stereotyping:

A widely held, preconceived and oversimplified assumption, label, image or idea of a particular type of person, especially about a group of people! Many stereotypes are racist, sexist, ageist, or homophobic. (See labeling, prejudice, fool's gold, fear, F.E.A.R., and Stinkin' Thinkin')

Stinkin' Thinkin'™:

A choice of negative and uncool thinkin' that can result in negative and hurtful consequences. *"Hey! That's Not OK!"™* (See Thinkin' Cap, P.U. Shoe, uncool, bullying, fear, F.E.A.R., prejudice, hate, fool's gold, and Claimjumper Pakk Ratts)

TCL™ / Treasure Chest Of Life:

A real or imagined container for the most valuable treasures in the universe, especially treasures that are greater than gold, like friendship, kindness, love, family, honesty, and most of all, you! (See treasure, treasure quest, treasure hunting, and gold)

Thinkin' Cap™:

The valuable real estate space, located between your ears inside your head. It houses the control-station in your head and is called your brain, It's where you manage your thinking, emotions, and make choices. (See cool Thinkin', Positive Thinkin' Stinkin' Thinkin', and choice)

Thumbs Up:

A hand signal to motion to others that you're okay. "Yes! I'm A-OK!"

Time / Time Travel:

"You never know what you'll find, when you travel back in time..."™ Traveling through past, present, and future times, by imagination or memory. Going on Vippi Mouse Treasure Quest expeditions through the Imagicadabra portals, to explore and travel through time, into the past, present, or future. The science fiction action of traveling through time. (See Imagicadabra, treasure quests, Vippi Treasure Quest Show and Vippiology)

Travel / Traveling:

A journey, quest, or expedition, to go from one place to another.

Treasure:

Something of great worth or value. A person esteemed as rare or precious. Wealth of any kind or in any form. A collection of precious things. A *Very Important Power*, Person, or Place. (See love, VIP, gold, nugget, treasure quest, and TCL).

Treasure Hunter / Hunting:

A Vippiologist who goes on quests searching for treasures and answers to questions. (See Expert-Expert, explorer, treasure quests, prospector, navigator, investigator, treasure, and TCL)

Treasure Quests:

Vippi's quest is to inspire people to discover the most valuable treasure in the universe, THEMSELVES. The treasure that is greater than gold!"™ Adventures, quests, searches, or expeditions to find things of great worth or value. (See treasure hunter, prospector, treasure, quests, solutions, investigator, and TCL Treasure)

Unacceptable:

Any choice, action, or behavior that is the result of Stinkin' Thinkin' (See bullying, Stinkin' Thinkin', uncool, Claim-Jumper Pakk Ratts, hate, prejudice, and P.U. Shoe)

Uncool:

Doing or saying something that puts someone else down or results in causing harm and damage. Cowardly, unacceptable, fake, and not accepted as cool, good, or proper. (See unacceptable, hate, prejudice, Compass Of Cool, Stinkin' Thinkin', and bullying)

Upstander / Upstanding:
An everyday hero, who is considerate of others, and uses his/her powers of voice and choice, to stand up for anyone or anything (including themselves), who are being hurt or bullied. They are courageous, and whenever they see any power imbalance, or injustice, upstanders use the powers of kindness, empathy and their voice to speak up for what is right, and to protect and support others. *"Hey! That's Not Okay!"*™ *"Hey! Are you OK?"* (See power, kindness, courage, leader, love, hero, Positive Thinkin', Cool Thinkin', inner compass, Compass Of Cool, excellent choices, heart, Expert-Expert, cool, empathy, considerate, compassion, and TCL).

Varmint:
A troublesome and mischievous person or wild animal. (See Claimjumper Pakk Ratts, bully, P.U. Shoe, hater, and Stinkin' Thinkin')

Very Important Person / Power / Place:
The greatest powers in the universe which include voice, choice, love, courage, gratitude, honesty, empathy, compassion, creativity, kindness, Cool Thinkin', voice, wisdom, imagination, friendship, being considerate of others, and on and on into timeless infinity! (See VIP, TCL, and Treasure)

V.I.P.:
A Very Important Person, Power, Place, and sometimes a Very Important Problem and solution. Everyone is a VIP and matters in this world. VIP's can make a positive difference in the world, through their choices. (See Vippi and Very Important Power)

Vippigram™:
Vippi's trademark personalized letters, postcards, and online message center to communicate with kids, treasure hunters, and Expert-Experts.

Vippiologist™:
Vippi Mouse and his Expert-Expert treasure hunters explore and study Vippiology. They have a special language of magic and treasure hunting. They have a unique way of looking at the universe and describing the world around them. Through the study of Vippiology you will come to understand that all that glitters isn't gold and that there are riches that are greater than even you can imagine. (See Vippi Mouse, Wild West Wendy Jo, Vippiology, Imagicadabra, Expert-Expert, treasure hunter, treasure quest, quest, explorer, VIP, investigator, Expert-Expert Treasure Hunter's Code Of Ethics, and The Compass Of Cool)

Vippiology™:
A study of Vippi Mouse Treasure Quests, research, investigations, and navigations into the greatest treasures in the universe. As Expert-Expert Vippiologists, we have our own guide and set of rules, called the *Expert-Expert Treasure Hunter's Code of Ethics™* It is a code of ethics poster which outlines the mission and values of Expert-Expert treasure hunters, based on the Compass Of Cool, and the upstanding way we are supposed to approach problems and behave.

Expert-Experts use Cool Thinkin' in making ethical and good choices, to maintain our core values and good standards to which the Vippiology Expert-Expert treasure hunting professional is held. (See Expert-Expert, Vippiology, Compass Of Cool, Cool Thinkin', treasure hunter, investigator, navigator, explorer, upstander, leader, time travel, and choice).

Vippi Code™:
Vippi's special brand of powerful code words and phrases that have unique meanings are Trademarks ™ of Vippiology and Vippi Treasure Quests. (See Expert-Expert Code of Ethics, Glossary and words and phrases with a ™ Trademark symbol)

Vippi Dance:
A dance that Vippi invented, where you high-five each other and dance like a rowdy bunch of prospectors who have just struck gold!

Vippi Mouse aka Vippi™:
A VIP Private Investigator and Treasure Hunting Navigator Mouse. The acronyms for Vippi are VIP; Very Important Person, Power, or Place, and P.I.; Private Investigator. *Vippi Mouse is on a quest to help kids discover the most valuable treasures in the Universe – like **themselves**, the treasure that is greater than gold.* (See Investigator, Navigator, and VIP)

Vippi Treasure Quest Show / Vippi Treasure Quests™:
Video and TV episodes of Vippi and Wild West Wendy Jo's Treasure Quest adventures in Vippiology, and guiding children to discover the most valuable treasures in the universe – like themselves, the treasure that is greater than gold. Video episodes of adventures, quests, searches, or expeditions to find things of great worth or value. (See Treasure Quests, Treasure Hunting, Vippiology, Imagicadabra, and time travel)

Voice:
A Very Important Power and freedom to stand up for yourself and others, and to express and communicate your opinions and beliefs. Wendy Jo and Vippi's motto, *"You Have a Choice – The Power of Voice"*™ *"Hey! That's Not Okay!"*™ (See leader, upstander, choice, power, Very Important Power, cool, Thinkin' Cap, proactive, action, courage, and hero)

Wild West Wendy Jo™ aka Wendy Jo:
A red-headed singing treasure hunter, whose Expert-Expert Power is her voice. Wendy Jo has lived in Utah, Wyoming, Arizona, Idaho, and New Mexico. She enjoys TCL treasure hunting, exploring and singing. She prefers wearing cowboy boots and a cowboy hat. She explores the wild west alongside her best friend, Vippi the treasure hunting navigator mouse. (See friend, voice, Vippiologist, TCL, Expert-Expert, upstander, cool, explorer, treasure hunter, treasure quests, navigator, and prospector)

You Have The Power:
A song about the very important powers of voice and kindness, written and recorded by Wild West Wendy Jo aka Wendy Jo Bradshaw.

ABOUT THE AUTHOR

Author/Illustrator/Storyteller/Singer/Songwriter/Treasure Hunter

Wendy Jo Bradshaw, more aptly described by her pen name Wild West Wendy Jo, is a feisty, red-headed, cowboy-boot wearing tomboy, who only experienced ONE boring day in her life. On that humdrum day, at twelve years old, she decided to NEVER be bored again!

As the oldest of four children, moving to many new schools throughout the West, Wendy Jo was the "New Kid", more times than she could count. Being an outsider trying to fit in, she was considered a misfit, by most of her classmates. As such, she quickly learned that she was a prime target of the schoolyard bullies. Wendy Jo was never one to run. Instead, she stood up to bullies, and even defended other kids from anyone who tried to steal their power. Those events, forever influenced her thoughts and dreams, and set in motion the idea to help kids find the power of their voice, and to feel powerful and good about themselves in spite of intimidation from anyone.

When not at school, Wendy Jo loved singing, playing the piano, spending time with her dog, and exploring. She spent much of her time organizing treasure hunting expeditions with her brothers and the other neighborhood renegades. She learned not only about the rewards of treasure hunting, but the perils, pitfalls, and the perseverance required in searching for treasures of all kinds.

Today, Wendy Jo still loves adventure and treasure hunting, and now teaches it to her children, grandchildren, and in schools to other people's kids! After surviving Stage III Melanoma cancer, she especially appreciates the hunt for treasures from the treasure chest of life (TCL), which are far more valuable than gold. Through that journey, she learned that the power of *choice* was one of the valuable treasures that helped save her life. Wendy continues to enjoy gold panning, metal detecting, fishing, and exploring ghost towns and historic ruins. Her dreams of helping children have become a reality. Wendy Jo uses her gifts of writing, singing and exploring to do what she loves most; creating empowering books, music, the Vippi Mouse Kid's show, and doing school presentations through her Vippi Mouse program. Wendy Jo's motto is: *Helping Kids See, They Are a Treasured VIP*. Oh, and since she was 12 years old, she's never been bored ONCE!

In conclusion here's a quote by Wild West Wendy Jo, that sums up her thoughts about the Treasure Chest of Life, *"When you hit rock bottom, remember, bedrock is where you find the gold!"*™

Wendy Jo now lives in Utah very near her children and grandchildren, with her spouse and two little Dachshunds named Annie Oakley and Jackpot. Wendy Jo is an award-winning author, illustrator, and singer, and is excited to finally debut her first solo children's book titled *A Very Important Power*. Wendy Jo's previous five books are a series of personalized books that she hired an author and illustrators to collaborate with. She belongs to the Society of Children's Book Writers and Illustrators, and is also an ally, and member of the Mama Dragons.

Here's a photo of eleven year old *Misfit Me* and my renegade brothers when we lived in Arizona. We were a working class family, but mysteriously, our parents were able to rent this house with a swimming pool, really cheap! More about that later.

About Vippi Mouse: The VIP Investigator and Treasure Hunting Navigator

"VIPPI HELPS KIDS SEE, THEY ARE A TREASURED VIP!"

Who is Vippi Mouse?
Vippi Mouse is a VIP Investigator, and treasure hunting navigator. He owns a magic, time traveling magnifying glass called the Imagicadabra. He's on a quest with sidekick Wild West Wendy Jo, to guide children on adventures through the portals of the Imagicadabra, to discover valuable treasures and riches that are even greater than gold such as friendship, kindness, courage, and most of all, themselves.

What are Vippi Treasure Quests?
Expeditions, investigations, and adventures in the mysteries of Vippiology, which is Vippi Code for all kinds of treasure hunting. Kids can discover gold, and riches that are greater than gold, like friendship, problem solving, kindness, courage, and most of all, themselves. They may even run into things like fool's gold, claim jumpers, and other problems, while Vippi guides them to find solutions through their power of choice.

What is Vippiology?
Vippi has a special language of magic and treasure hunting. He has a unique way of looking at the universe and describing the world around him. Through Vippiology you will come to understand that all that glitters isn't gold and that there are riches that are greater than you can even imagine.

SPECIAL THANKS
Loving thanks to my family, especially my children, grandchildren, and spouse, for their influence in writing this book, and for being the treasure I value most.

Huge gratitude and thanks to my *friend* Al Jim Reese, who showed me the true, unconditional meaning of *friendship*! Al, thank you for believing in me and Vippi Mouse, from the very beginning!

Thanks to digital illustrator Tobias White, for seeing my vision, and helping me get my paper sketches, complex book design, and my original characters, transformed into beautiful digital illustrations! Thanks to Morgan Crockett for final editing, book formatting, and dust jacket design, Waldinei Lafaiete for book cover, formatting, and graphic design, Skylar Avila for Photoshop editing, Lee Steadman for photograph of Wild West Wendy Jo, and the late Jerry Pointak for helping me design the character Vippi Mouse.

Thanks to all the artists who have inspired me, including Mom, Dad, Carol Burnette, Barbra Streisand, J.K. Rowling, and most of all, a lifetime of thanks to **Barry Manilow** for the piano, and inspiring me to write music, and to never give up on my dreams.

Last but not least, I want to thank all of you who helped proofread, edit, review, photograph, website design, and promote this book. Thanks to all of my family and friends including Evelyn Garlington for your support, patience, proofreading, and suggestions, Dante, Kiara, Shante, Brenda, Coral Mangus, Hazel Weight, Lor Bingham, Jay Fleming, Rostin Walker, Cinda Gibb, Amy Bevan, A.A. Callister Corp, Vippi's Street Team, and all the other VIP's that helped!

Vippi Mouse Theme Song ©2019
(Listen to it at www.vippimouse.com)

"Vippi Mouse the VIP Investigator,
Vippi Mouse the Treasure Hunting Navigator,
on the quest for Gold n Nuggets in the West.
Searching for treasures of the nicest kind,
what you prize makes a difference in your life.
On the quest, traps and troubles you may find.
You will know when you have hit the Mother lode.
Don't be fooled cuz' all that glitters isn't gold.
Vippi Mouse is the name, treasure finding's the game. Ahh…"

If you enjoyed reading this, please take a few moments to leave a review or email me with your feedback from our website vippimouse.com. I love to hear from readers!

GET MORE FROM THE STORY! For FREE SONGS, downloads, and write a letter to Vippi Mouse or Wild West Wendy Jo, go to www.vippimouse.com

COMING SOON! Watch more adventures in the *Treasure Quests* series.

From our website and the following links, you can watch the *Vippi Treasure Quest Show*, write a *Vippigram* letter or email to Vippi Mouse, watch for our next book in the series, and get free downloads and updates about Vippi & Wild West Wendy Jo's Treasure Quests.

www.vippimouse.com
www.youtube.com/vippimouse
www.facebook.com/vippimouse
www.instagram.com/vippimouse
www.instagram.com/wildwestwendyjo
www.pinterest.com/vippimouse
www.twitter.com/wendybradshaw
www.twitter.com/VIPPI_BOOKS
www.wildwestwendyjo.com

———————

Illustrated by Tobias White and Wendy Jo Bradshaw

Library of Congress Control Number: 2019900964
ISBN 978-1-7327789-2-4
First Edition Printed in China

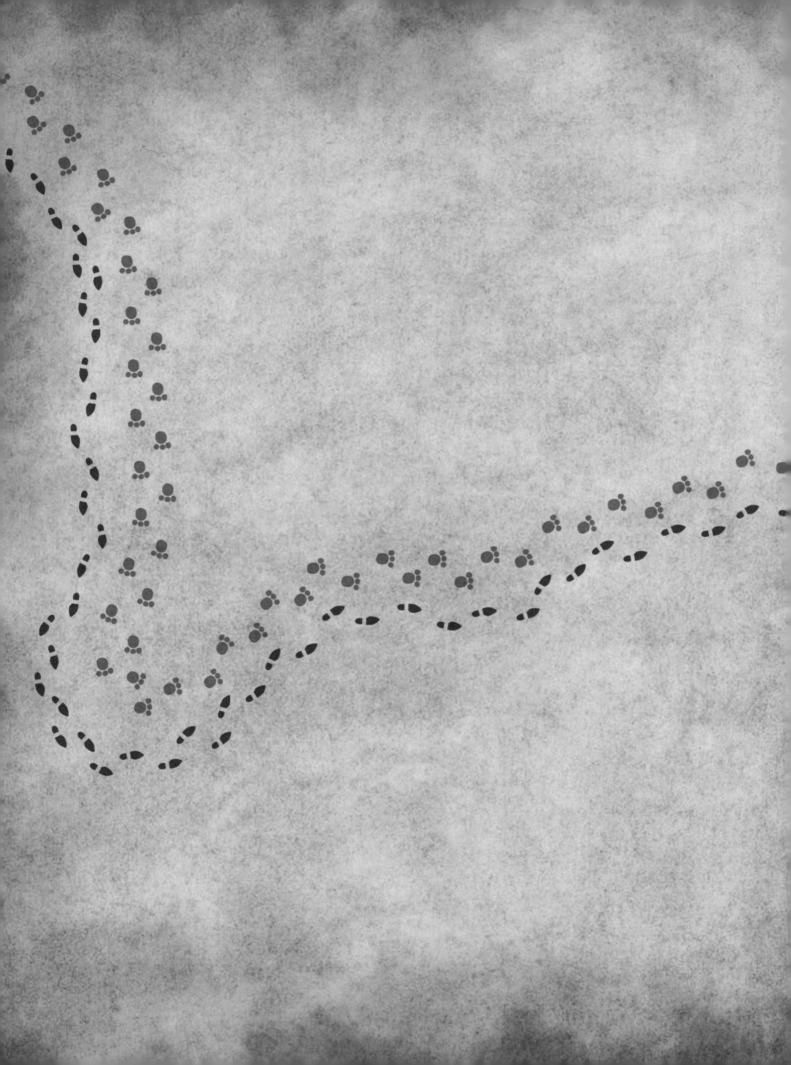